Sam Sunday and the Strange Disappearance of Chester Cats

Parents' Magazine Press · New York

Sam Sunday and the Strange Disappearance of Chester Cats

story *by* ROBYN SUPRANER
pictures *by* ROBERT TALLON

Text copyright © 1978 by Robyn Supraner
Illustrations copyright © 1978 by Robert Tallon
Printed in the United States of America
10 9 8 7 6 5 4 3 2 1

Library of Congress Cataloging in Publication Data

Supraner, Robyn.
   Sam Sunday and the strange disappearance
of Chester Cats.

   SUMMARY: The best detective on the police force
searches for Mrs. Cats' missing son.
   [1. Mystery and detective stories. 2. Cats—
Fiction] I. Tallon, Robert, 1939-   II. Title.
PZ7.S9652Sam   [E]   78-11062
ISBN 0-1893-0993-1   ISBN 0-8193-0994-X

For Gladys Barbara Banks
and Bobbe Salkowitz...
my friend.

Sam Sunday and the Strange Disappearance of Chester Cats

Chester Cats was missing. His mother was very upset.

"Where can my Chester be?" she cried. "I miss him. Lolly and Polly miss him. Dicky and Ricky miss him. Terry, Merry and Melvin miss him. The house is empty without him!"

She baked a salmon pie, and wrote CHESTER on the crust.   Then she went to the window.

"Yoo hoo!" she called.   "Chester, come home for lunch!   Your salmon pie is getting cold!"

When Chester did not come, she decided to call the police.

Officer Klink answered the phone. Mrs. Cats told him about Chester.

"Don't worry," said Officer Klink. "We will put our best man on the case."

At one o'clock the doorbell rang. Mrs. Cats opened the door.

"Good afternoon, ma'am. I am Sam Sunday. I am a detective."

"Come in, come in," said Mrs. Cats. "Give me your raincoat and have a cup of tea."

"No thank you, ma'am," said Sam. "I never drink on the job." He opened a little black book and said, "Tell me, Mrs. Cats, when did you last see your son?"

"Just before breakfast," she said. "I always say a growing child needs a good hot breakfast. I get up at six o'clock every morning..."

"Just the facts, ma'am," said Sam.

Mrs. Cats patted her apron. "Breakfast was on the table," she said. "I called Chester, but he didn't answer."

"Why was that, ma'am?" asked Sam.

"Because he was gone!" cried Mrs. Cats. She took out a handkerchief and blew her nose.

"There, there," said Sam. "Don't worry, ma'am. Big Sam is here to help you."

Mrs. Cats stopped crying. She took a sip of tea.

"Does your son have any hobbies?" asked Sam.

"He reads," said Mrs. Cats. "My Chester loves to read."

Sam nodded his head. He wrote in his book.

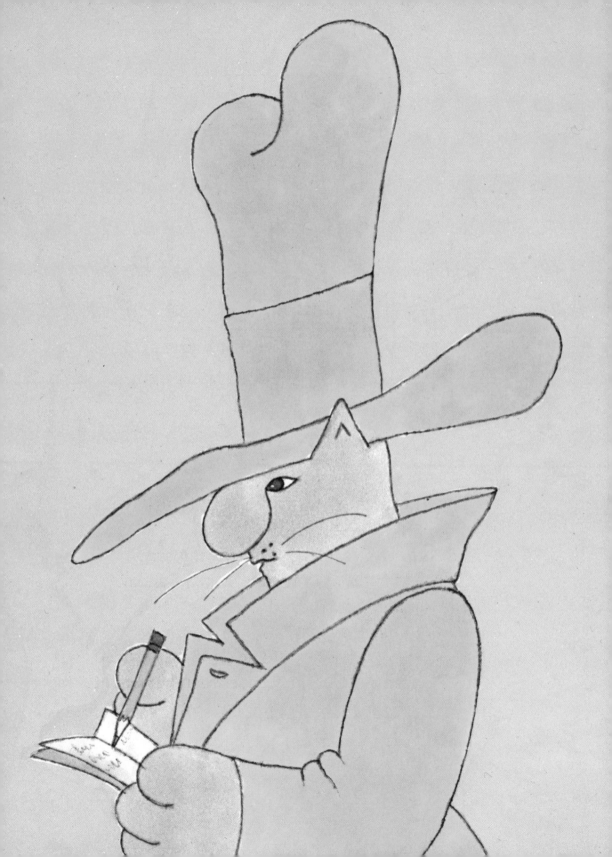

Then he pointed to a picture. "Is that your son?" he asked.

"Yes," said Mrs. Cats. "That is my son."

"What's that in his left ear?" asked Sunday.

"An earring," she replied.

"An earring?" said Sunday.

"Yes," said Mrs. Cats. "One day, Chester read a story about a gypsy cat. That's when he bought the earring. He wanted to be a gypsy, too."

"I see," said Sam. "Is there anything else you can tell me about Chester?"

"He loves fish," said Mrs. Cats. All kinds of fish—sardines, salmon, codfish, tuna..."

"That's enough, ma'am. I get the picture."

"One more thing," said Mrs. Cats. "Chester is crazy about animals—hamsters, rabbits, chickens, mice..."

"Enough!" said Sam. "I will find your son or my name is not Sam Sunday!"

Sam got into his car.

"If Chester is crazy about animals," he said, "I know just the place to find him."

He drove to the zoo.

"I am looking for a cat," he told the zoo keeper.

"We have a lot of cats," said the zoo keeper.

Sam Sunday shook his head. "He doesn't have a mane or a tassle on his tail. He doesn't have spots. He doesn't have stripes either."

"What *does* he have?" asked the zoo keeper.

"An earring," said Sam. "He has an earring in his left ear."

"An earring?" said the zoo keeper.

"You heard me," said Sam.

"Sorry," said the zoo keeper. "Try another zoo."

Sam drove away. "If Chester loves to read," he said, "I know just the place to find him."

He drove to the library and parked his car. Then he went to find the librarian.

A sign on the librarian's desk said: TICKLE, TILLIE.

"Good afternoon, ma'am," said Sam. "Would you like a big tickle or a little tickle?"

"Fresh!" snapped the librarian. She hit Sam with a book. "For your information," she said, "that sign says Tickle *comma* Tillie. Tickle is my last name."

"A thousand pardons!" said Sam Sunday. "I am Sunday *comma* Sam and I'm looking for a cat."

"We have a lot of cats," said Tillie. "We have *The Cat in the Hat* and *The Three Little Kittens*. We have *Puss in Boots*..."

"Enough!" said Sam. "You don't understand. I'm not looking for a book about cats. I'm looking for a cat who loves books."

"That's different," said the librarian. "What does this cat of yours look like?"

"Gray coat. Yellow eyes. Gold earring in left ear," said Sam.

"Sorry," said Tillie. "I have not seen your gypsy cat."

Sam Sunday got back in his car. "Hmmm," he said. "Tillie Tickle has given me a very good idea!"

Sam drove past tall buildings. He drove past small buildings. He drove past farms and chickens and cows. At last, he came to a place where blue smoke curled up from a green wood.

"Where there's smoke, there's fire," said Sam. He parked his car and went into the woods.

He walked and walked. After a while, he heard music and laughter.

A band of gypsies was sitting around a camp-fire. A little gypsy sat with them. A golden earring dangled from the tip of his left ear!

"Sorry to spoil the party, folks," said Sam. "This little gypsy is going home."

"Do not touch Carmello!" cried a beautiful gypsy. "Carmello is mine. He is my morning light! He is my evening star!"

"This is no gypsy, ma'am," said Sam. "This is Chester Cats. Coat, gray. Eyes, yellow. Gold earring in left ear."

"Dummy!" cried the beautiful gypsy. "Carmello's earring is in his right ear!"

"Oops!" said Sam. "That's a fact, ma'am."

"I will help you anyway," said the beautiful gypsy.

She gazed into her crystal ball.

"I see a little cat," she said. "His coat is gray. His eyes are yellow. He is wearing an earring in his *left* ear..."

"That's Chester, ma'am," said Sam.

"Shhhhh!" said the beautiful gypsy. "Do not interrupt! I see water. I see fish. Sardines, salmon, codfish..."

"That's enough, ma'am," said Sam. "I get the picture."

He thanked the beautiful gypsy. He shook hands with Carmello. "If Chester is with all those fish," he said, "I know just the place to find him."

He drove past cows and chickens and farms. He drove past small buildings. He drove past tall buildings. At last he came to a sign that said:

WELCOME TO THE AQUARIUM

A crowd was watching the fish. At the edge of the crowd, stood a little cat. He had a gray coat and yellow eyes.

"Chester Cats?" said Sam Sunday.

The little cat turned around. A golden earring dangled from the tip of his left ear.

"I am Chester Cats," he said.

"I'm taking you home," said Sam Sunday. "Your mother is worried about you."

"My mother is always worried about me," said Chester. "Why is she worried today?"

"She doesn't know where you are," said Sam.

"I know where I am," said Chester. "There's nothing to worry about."

"She thinks you're lost," said Sam.

"I'm not lost," said Chester. "I'm right here, in the aquarium."

"Enough!" said Sam. "Get into the car!"

When they got to Chester's house, Mrs. Cats was at the door. So were Lolly, Polly, Dicky, Ricky, Terry, Merry and Melvin.

Everyone was happy to see Chester.

They hugged him and kissed him and kissed him and hugged him.

"I wasn't lost," said Chester.

Mrs. Cats hugged Sam Sunday.

"Have a bite with us," she said. "We're having sardine stew and kidney pie, herring hash and codfish cakes, liver soup..."

"Enough!" said Sam. "That's nice of you, ma'am. I don't mind if I do."

And he did.

About the Author:

Robyn Supraner is well known as the author of several successful picture-book stories including *Giggly, Wiggly and Snickety-Snick* published by Parents' Magazine Press. She has been a lyricist, has taught creative dramatics, and is at present teaching a course in writing for children in Roslyn, New York where she and her family live.

About the Artist:

Robert Tallon has done many covers for *The New Yorker*, and is the author-illustrator of such popular picture books as *Fish Story, Zoophabets,* and *Little Cloud* for Parents' Magazine Press. He has designed and written films for Sesame Street and his paintings have been exhibited both in one-man and group shows at leading galleries and museums throughout the United States. Mr. Tallon lives in New York City.